BIG ISLAND
ACTIVITY BOOK

Shirley Hasenyager

Illustrated by Barbara Downs

Even if you can't visit all the places described in this

book, we hope you have fun solving the puzzles.

The answers are at the back of the book.

Copyright © 1996 by The Bess Press, Inc.
P. O. Box 22388, Honolulu, Hawai'i 96823
ALL RIGHTS RESERVED
Printed in the United States of America
ISBN: 1–57306–018–6

Hawai'i, the Big Island

The Big Island has five volcanoes: Mauna Loa, Kīlauea, Mauna Kea, Kohala, and Hualālai. **Find these volcanoes on the map below.**

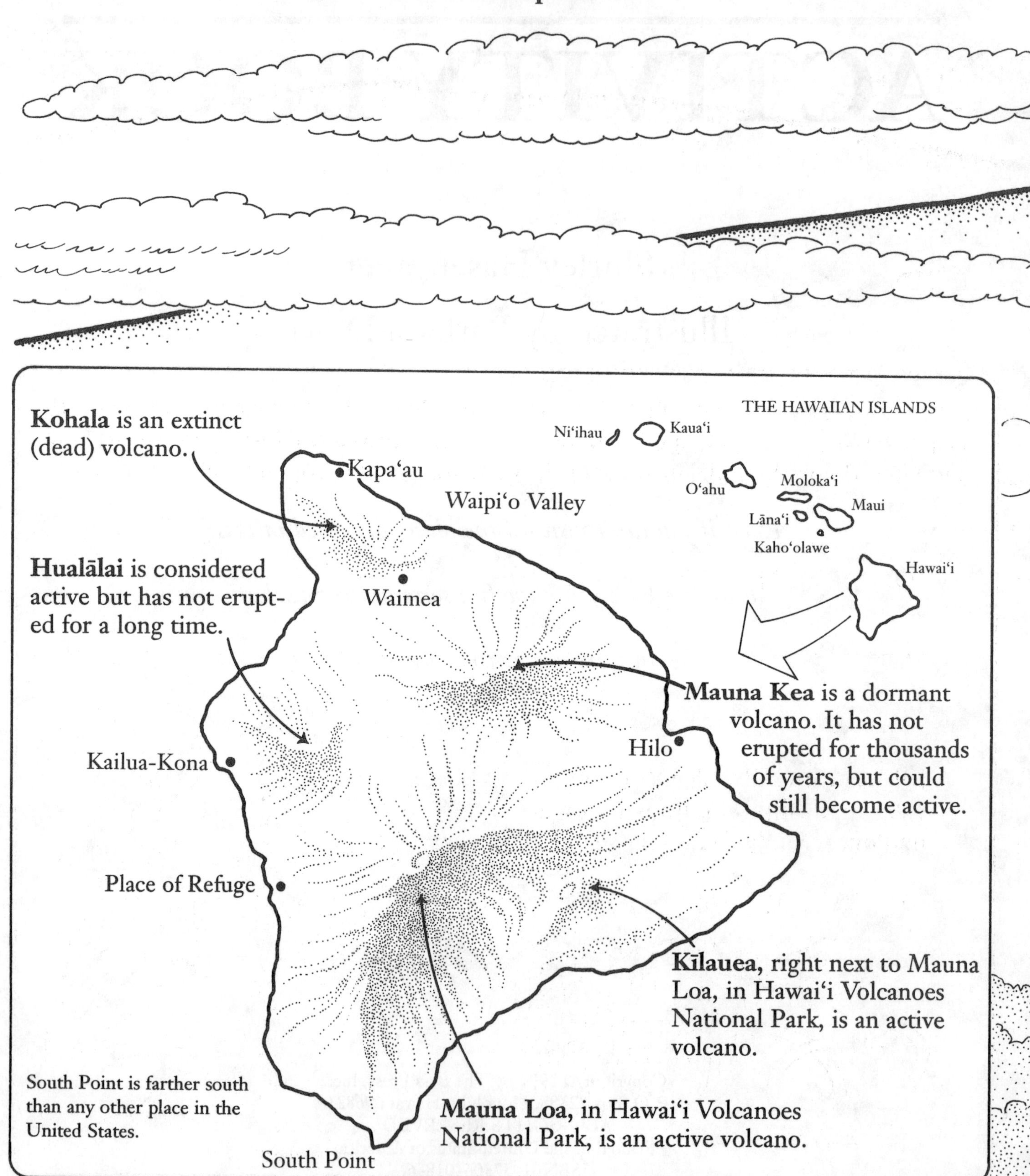

Mauna Loa and Kīlauea

Mauna Loa is 13,680 feet above sea level. It is called a shield volcano because of its shape, made by the gradual slope of its sides. **Unscramble the letters below** to find out what Mauna Loa means in English (its shape should give you a clue).

O G N L   O N T N A U M I

_ _ _ _ _   _ _ _ _ _ _ _

Kīlauea is the Big Island's youngest volcano. **Follow the lines below** to find out what "Kīlauea" means.

W P E N G S I

_ _ _ _ _ _ _

Kīlauea Caldera

Use the 12 letters from the Hawaiian alphabet below to find the name of the big crater inside Kīlauea Caldera.

A	H	E	I	K	L	M	N	O	P	U	W
1	2	3	4	5	6	7	8	9	10	11	12

_ _ _ _ _ _ _ _ _ _
2 1 6 3 7 1 11 7 1 11

Now **match the numbers and letters** again to learn what this name means in English.

E	H	S	R	U	F	O	N
1	2	3	4	5	6	7	8

_ _ _ _ _ _ _ _ _
6 1 4 8 2 7 5 3 1

The crater is also known as the home of Pele, the Hawaiian goddess of fire.

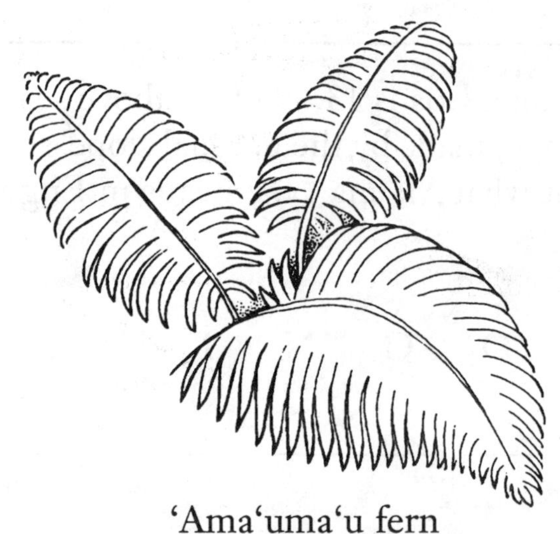

'Ama'uma'u fern

—— Look for these things around the caldera and crater ——

Around the crater and caldera (a very large crater) are many steam vents and sulphur vents. Sulphur is a yellow chemical that smells very bad. You will know when you are near a sulphur vent! Steam vents are caused by surface water seeping into cracks or holes in the ground. Hot volcanic rocks are several feet under the surface, and when the rain and mist seep down, steam is created.

Going around the caldera, watch for the sulphur banks and steaming bluffs. You might find _ʻōhelo_ berries and bamboo orchids at the bluffs.

Stop at the Jaggar Museum and make the seismometer move. Watch the seismographs record any movements of the Earth. Can you find a record of an earthquake?

Earthquake Trail

On November 16, 1983, an earthquake shook Hawai'i Volcanoes National Park so hard that some of the Kīlauea Caldera rim fell into the caldera, taking away some of the road and Crater Rim Trail.

Find the right earthquake trail that leads to the Visitor Center.

Nēnē

The *nēnē* is a native goose. It was almost extinct forty years ago and is still endangered. It is Hawai'i's state bird.

Help the *nēnē* find the right path through the smooth *pāhoehoe* lava to her nest in the grass.

Pua'a and *Hāpu'u*

The *pua'a* is a wild pig that eats plants and causes much damage in the rain forest. The *hāpu'u* (tree fern) is the biggest native fern in the forest. It has "hair" (*pulu*) that was once used for pillow stuffing. *Hāpu'u* grow under taller trees such as the *'ōhi'a*.

Find the shortest trail to get the *pua'a* out of the *hāpu'u* before it damages the plants. The *pueo* (Hawai'i's only native owl) and the *'io* (an endangered hawk found only on the Big Island) are watching.

Flowers and Berries

Follow the lines to the correct picture for each plant and write its name under the picture.

The *lehua* blossom is the flower of the native *'ōhi'a* tree. Legends say that if you pick a blossom going up the volcano, it will rain. Even if you're going downhill, don't pick the flowers. They provide food for native forest birds.

The pretty little bamboo orchid is not native to Hawai'i. It grows near the sulphur banks and steaming bluffs. The flower is purple, lavender, and white.

Mountain *naupaka* is a "half" flower with only five petals. It is usually white. The little fruits it forms are a very dark purple. There is also a *naupaka* at sea level. A legend says that two sweethearts were separated and one became the half flower at the ocean and the other in the mountains.

'Ōhelo berries grow on a low bush. The red berries are a favorite food of *nēnē*.

Three kinds of ginger plants grow in the volcanoes area: white, yellow and kāhili (also yellow). They are very pretty and have a wonderful scent. However, they multiply rapidly and are choking out the native forest plants.

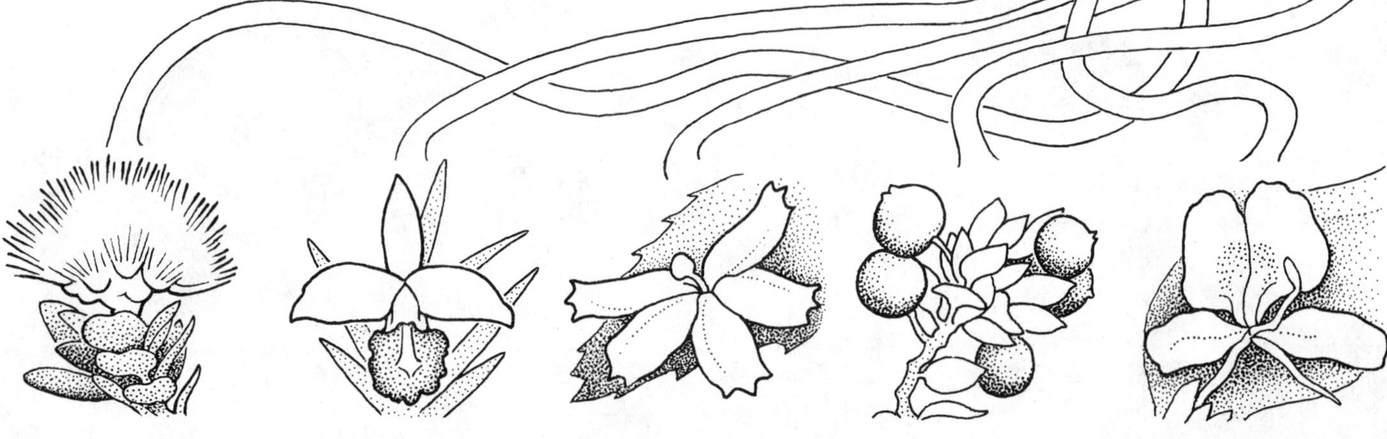

___________ ___________ ___________ ___________ ___________

___________ ___________ ___________ ___________ ___________

Kīpuka Puaulu

A *kīpuka* is a place that lava has not covered in recent history, so it has old trees and other plants.

The *koa* tree is a native Hawaiian tree important to native bird and insects.

Find 6 birds in the *koa* tree at Kīpuka Puaulu.

The leaves on a *koa* tree first look like ferns.

Ka'ū Desert Trail

Walk Ka'ū Desert Trail and see native plants, 400-year-old lava flows, and footprints Hawaiian warriors made when they walked through soft ash. The ash then hardened and preserved the footprints. Do not step on them. **Fill in the blanks** to spell 22 words from the letters in "footprints":

f __ __   This is found on a fish.

f __ __ __   The right size (The shoe f_ _ _.)

f __ __ __   You walk on these (singular).

n __ __   I will __ __ __ step on the footprints.

p __ __   Hole in the ground

p __ __   A big pan

p __ __ __ __   To write or stamp

p __ __ __ __   Evidence of truth or fact

r __ __   To tear apart

r __ __ __   Top of a house

r __ __ __   Part of a plant that is underground

r __ __   To decay or spoil

s __ __ __   Not hard or rough (A pillow is s _ _ _.)

s __ __   A boy is this to his father.

s __ __ __ __   To bend over

s __ __ __   To quit or halt

t __ __   Pointed end or to turn something over

t __ __   2000 pounds

t __ __ __   Noise from a horn or train

t __ __   Highest part of something

t __ __ __   A journey or to stumble

t __ __ __ __   A group of Scouts or soldiers

t __ __ __   Movement of a horse

Chain of Craters Road

Find the way from Kīlauea Caldera to the ocean down the Chain of Craters Road. **Count the craters** you pass on this road.

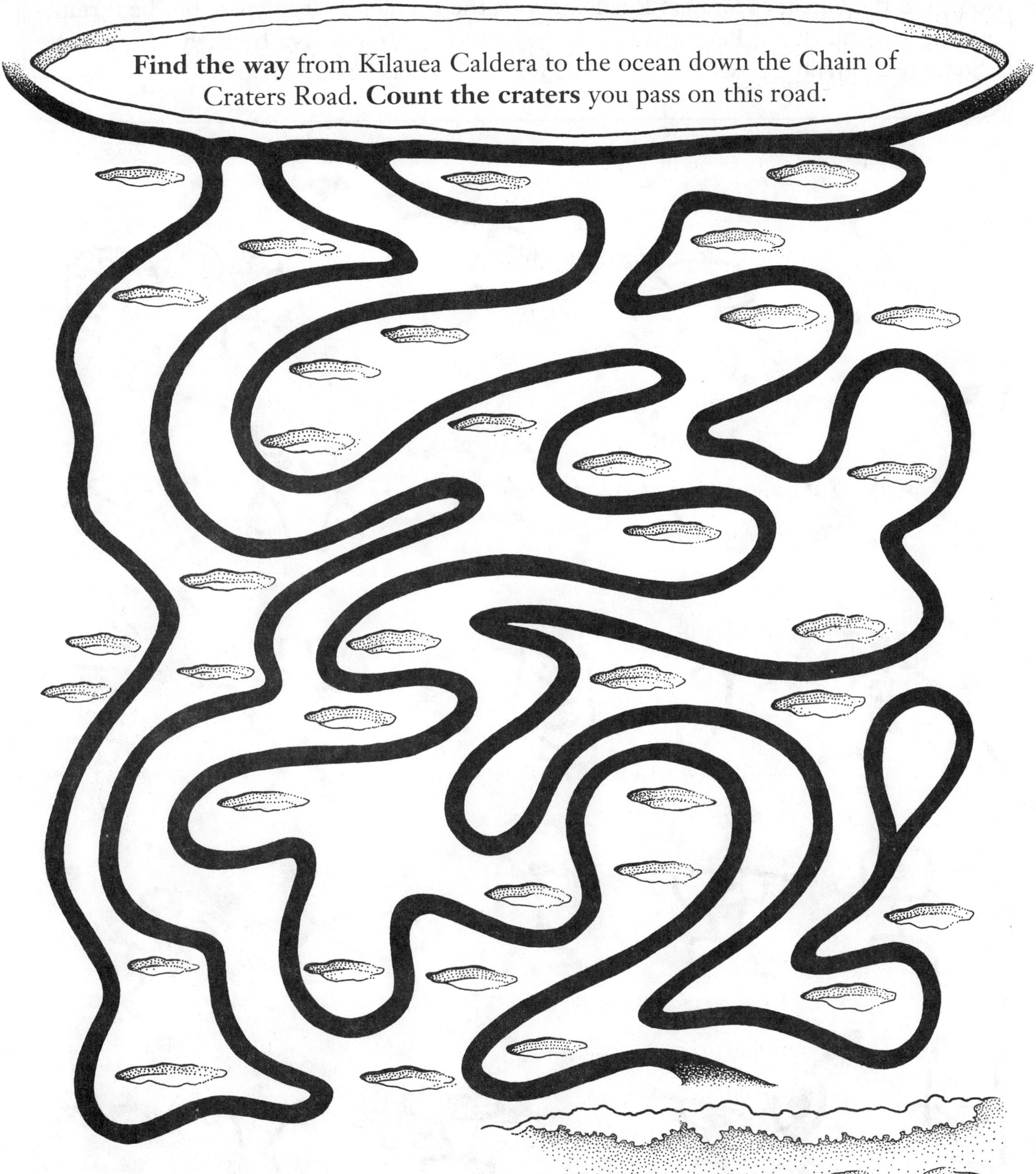

How many craters did you pass on the correct road? ____

Petroglyphs

Stop on the Chain of Craters Road and visit the Puʻuloa Petroglyphs, but be careful not to step on them. Petroglyphs are carvings in *pāhoehoe* lava by early Hawaiians. Some petroglyph figures are shown below. **Find 3 that are identical.**

Lava

Pāhoehoe lava is smooth-flowing and cools in smooth mounds and in ropy shapes.

ʻAʻā lava is jagged and rocky.

Lava trees and tree molds form when lava cools around trees, which then burn away, leaving either standing forms or holes.

Lava tubes form when surface lava cools, but hot lava continues flowing underneath. When it drains out, it leaves a cave or tube. "Magma" is the name for lava when it is still underground.

In the picture below are *pāhoehoe* and *ʻaʻā* lava and lava trees. **Hidden in the picture** are an *ʻōhiʻa lehua* blossom, a tree fern (*hāpuʻu*), a petroglyph, a footprint, a *nēnē*, and the words "lava," "*ʻaʻā*" and "*pāhoehoe*."

Can you find them?

What's What?

Draw a line to the correct picture.

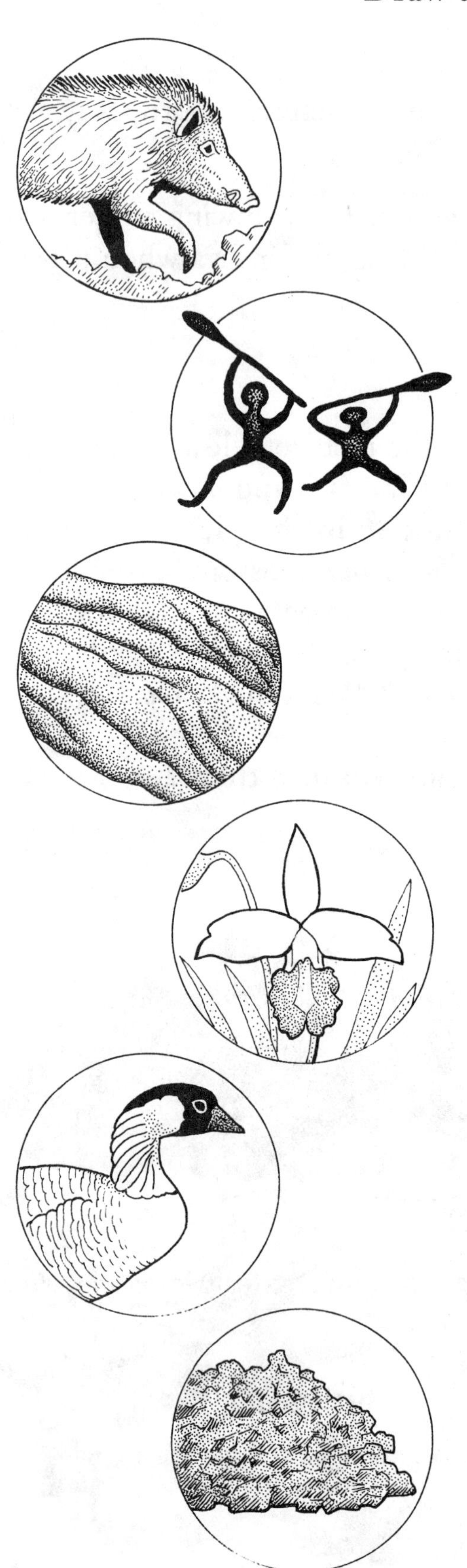

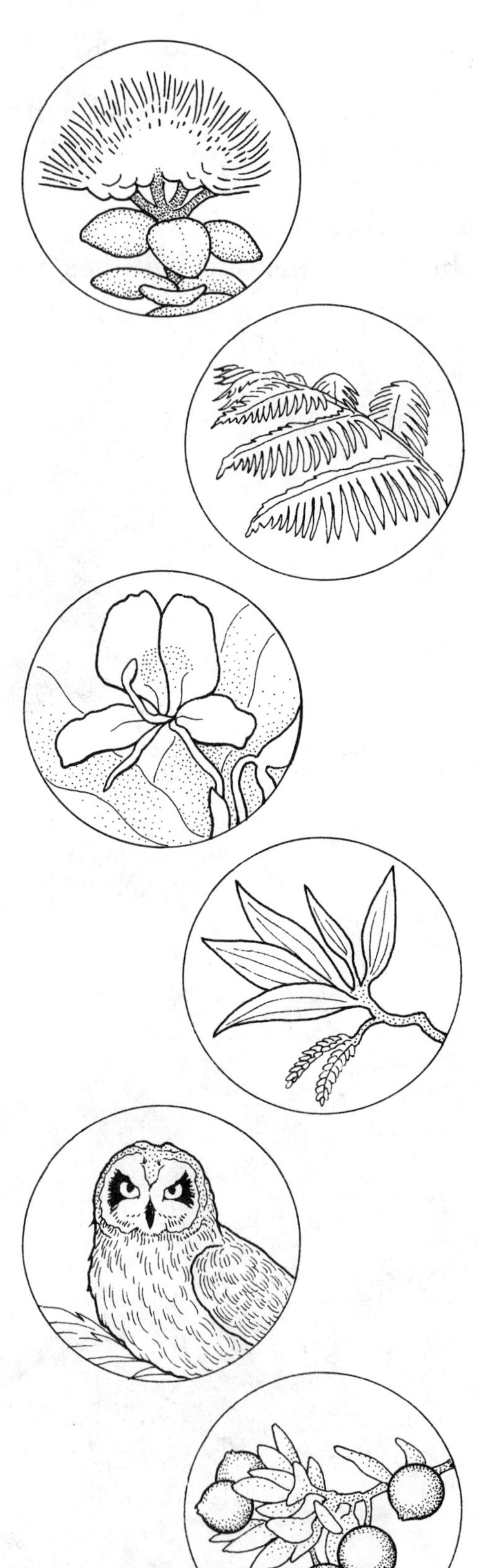

Petroglyphs

Koa tree leaves

Nēnē

Pāhoehoe lava

ʻŌhelo berries

ʻAʻā lava

ʻŌhiʻa lehua blossom

Puaʻa

Wild orchid

Pueo

Hāpuʻu tree fern

Ginger

Forest Puzzle

Across

1. Native tree with pretty wood used for canoes, furniture and bowls
3. Plant that grows in a rain forest
4. Red flower on the *'ōhi'a* tree
5. Hawaiian goose (state bird)
6. A lot of this is needed to make the forests grow.
9. Native tree that has red blossoms
10. A place that lava has not covered
11. Wild animals that dig up forest plants

Down

2. Red berries that grow in the volcano and are eaten by *nēnē*
3. Big group of trees
5. White flower that looks like a half flower
7. Tree fern
8. Hawaiian word for pig
9. Purple and lavender flower

15

Ka‘ū Desert Trail
Move ahead 2 spaces
Dead ‘ōhi‘a tree on trail
Go back 1 space
Pāhoehoe lava
covers trail
Go back 1 space
Devastation Trail Game
Don't step on the nēnē nest!
Move ahead 1 space
Steam vent. Ouch!
Go back 1 space
A pig (pua‘a) has
dug up the trail.
Go around 1 space
Stinky sulphur pit!
Move ahead 1 space

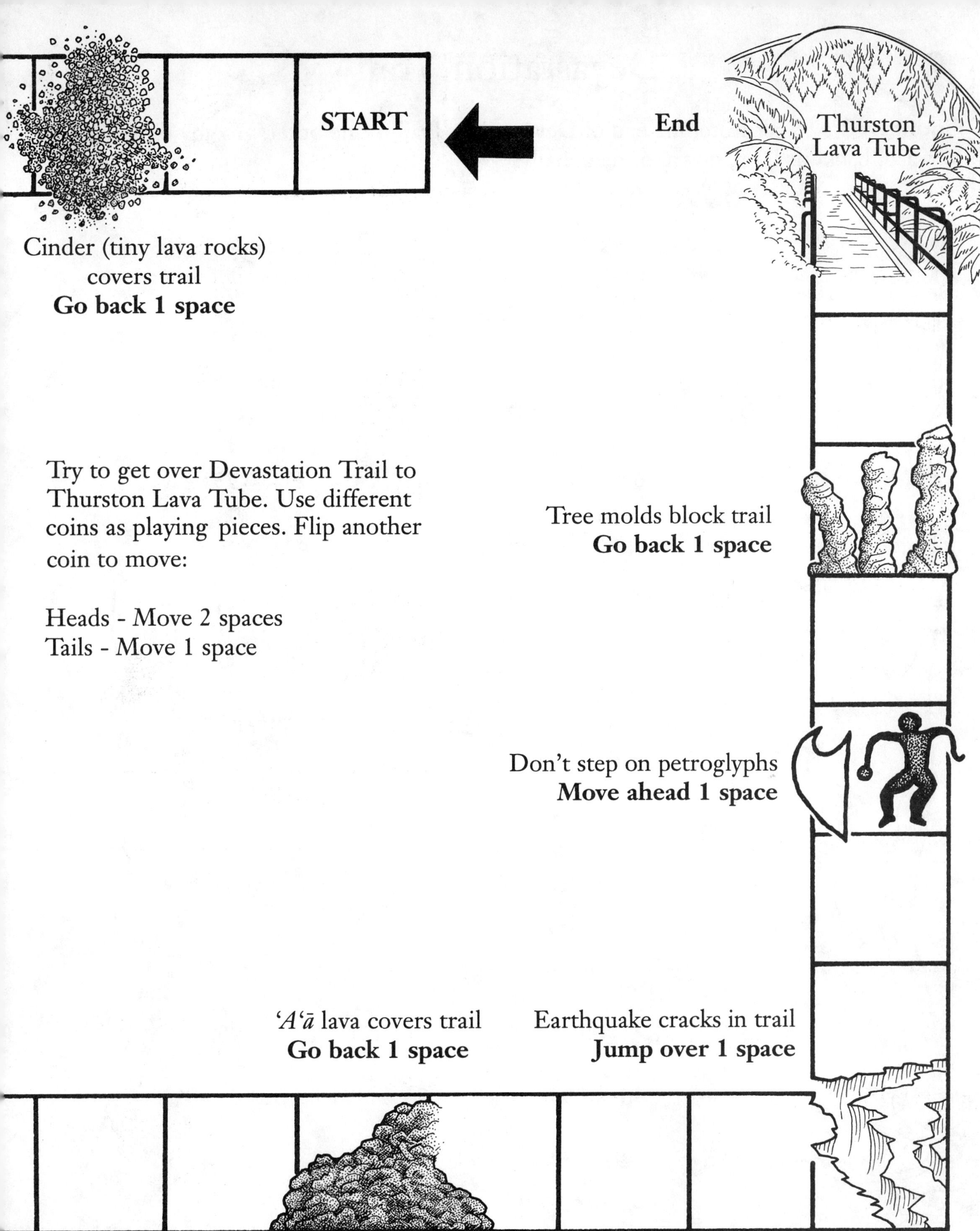

START

End

Thurston
Lava Tube

Cinder (tiny lava rocks)
covers trail
Go back 1 space

Try to get over Devastation Trail to
Thurston Lava Tube. Use different
coins as playing pieces. Flip another
coin to move:

Heads - Move 2 spaces
Tails - Move 1 space

Tree molds block trail
Go back 1 space

Don't step on petroglyphs
Move ahead 1 space

'A'ā lava covers trail
Go back 1 space

Earthquake cracks in trail
Jump over 1 space

Devastation Trail

Count by 3's to get from one end of Devastation Trail to the other. Go any direction— forward, backward, up, down, or diagonally.

Volcanoes Word Search

Find these words in the square below. They may be horizontal, vertical, diagonal, or backwards.

OHELO	CINDER	PUAA	LAVA
MAUNA KEA	PIG	ORCHID	KIPUKA
VENT	FERN	SULPHUR	VOLCANO
OHIA	KOA	RAIN	PELE
HAPUU	MAUNA LOA	NENE	AA
	FOREST	PETROGLYPH	

```
O L E H O C I N D E R
L A T P U A A E O U O
A V E E F E R N H M N
V E N T O T E P A E A
A M O R R T L E B A C
A U K O E U T U T O L
E P I G S S T A I H O
K O P L T O A K O A V
A R U Y V U R A I N O
N C K P K A O P E L E
U H A H A P U U V E N
A I T M A U N A L O A
M D S U P N E N E K A
```

Mauna Kea

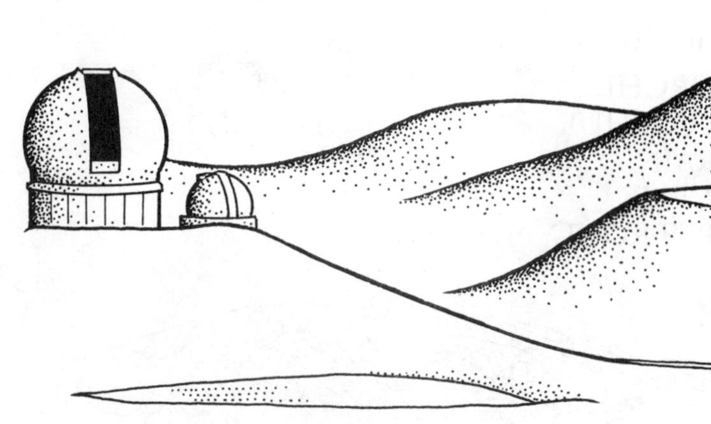

Puʻu Wēkiu, a cinder cone, is the summit of Mauna Kea at 13,796 feet. "Puʻu Wēkiu" means "summit" or "topmost hill."

Lake Waiau is a small lake at 13,020 feet. **Use the code below** to find out what "Waiau" means.

I	G	S	A	W	R	N	E	T	L
1	2	3	4	5	6	7	8	9	10

__ __ __ __ __ __ __ __
 3   5   1   6   10   1   7   2

__ __ __ __ __
 5   4   9   8   6

Because there is not much oxygen at the summit, astronomers live at **Hale Pōhaku** at 9200 feet and travel to the summit to use the oservatories' huge telescopes at night. **Use the chart below** to find out what "Hale Pōhaku" means.

	A	B	C	D	E
1	E	S	L	O	K
2	M	N	T	U	H

___ ___ ___ ___ ___
B1   C2   D1   B2   A1

___ ___ ___ ___ ___
E2   D1   D2   B1   A1

Mauna Kea is a major astronomy center, almost twice as high as other major astronomy centers. **Use the chart below** to find out what "Mauna Kea" means. Why do you think it was given this name?

	A	B	C	D	E	F	G	H
1	T	W	C	H	M	X	O	A
2	B	D	I	N	U	E	L	K

___ ___ ___ ___ ___
B1   D1   C2   A1   F2

___ ___ ___ ___ ___ ___ ___ ___
E1   G1   E2   D2   A1   H1   C2   D2

Star Path

Find the way to the moon from Mauna Kea. Count by 2's. Go backward, forward, or diagonally to connect the stars.

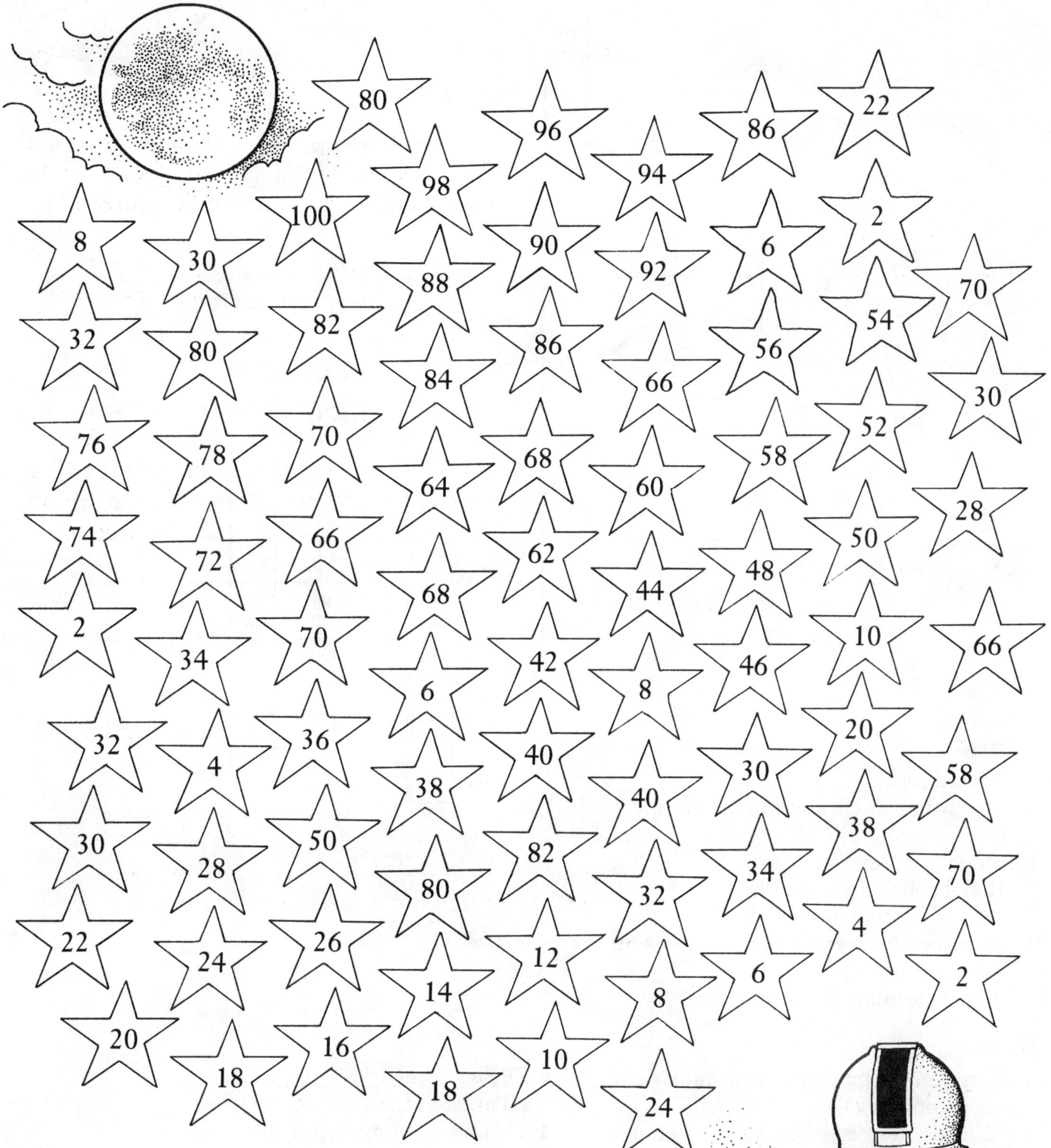

Volcano Crossword

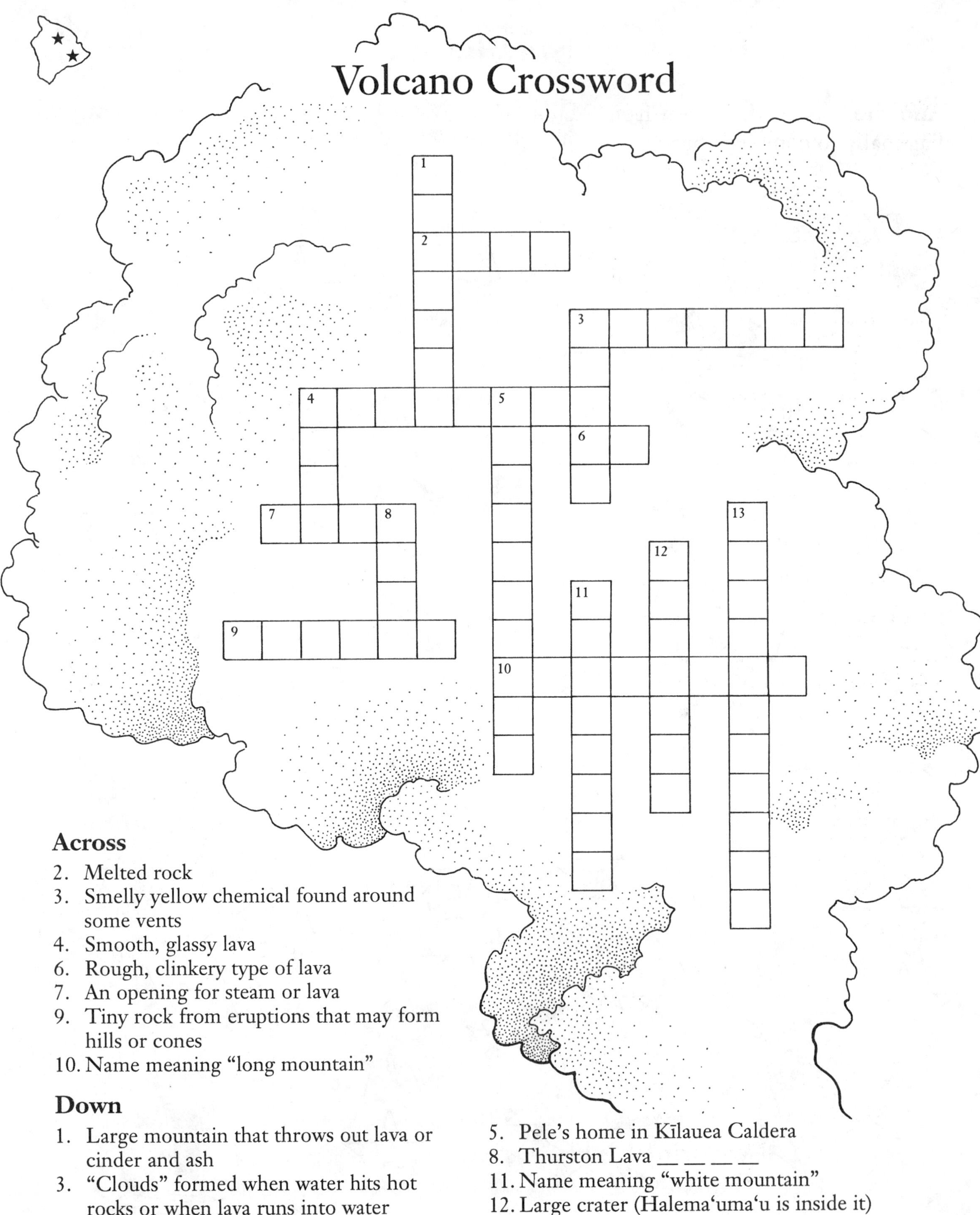

Across

2. Melted rock
3. Smelly yellow chemical found around some vents
4. Smooth, glassy lava
6. Rough, clinkery type of lava
7. An opening for steam or lava
9. Tiny rock from eruptions that may form hills or cones
10. Name meaning "long mountain"

Down

1. Large mountain that throws out lava or cinder and ash
3. "Clouds" formed when water hits hot rocks or when lava runs into water
4. Goddess of the volcano
5. Pele's home in Kīlauea Caldera
8. Thurston Lava __ __ __ __
11. Name meaning "white mountain"
12. Large crater (Halemaʻumaʻu is inside it)
13. Images carved into rocks

Hilo

Hilo is the government center of the Big Island. It is known for orchids, anthuriums, and macadamia nuts. Rainbow Falls is in Hilo, on the Wailuku River. Morning is the best time to see rainbows in the mists from the falls.

Find the Hawaiian word for "rainbow" from this code:

E N A U
1 2 3 4

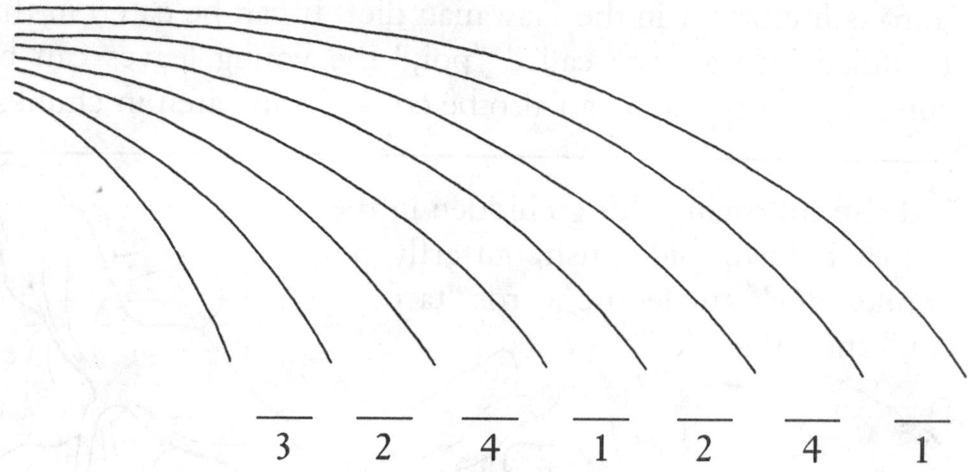

__ __ __ __ __ __ __
3 2 4 1 2 4 1

Farther up the river past Rainbow Falls are the boiling pots. They are a series of holes in the river that bubble like "boiling pots" when the flow of water is heavy.

Find and circle the following words. They may be horizontal, vertical, or upside down.

POTS   BOILING   FALLS   RIVER   ORCHIDS   ANTHURIUM
MACADAMIA   RAINBOW   NUTS   ANUENUE   HILO

A	N	T	H	U	R	I	U	M
W	A	W	T	H	I	L	O	A
A	P	O	T	S	V	S	R	C
N	E	B	R	S	E	T	C	A
U	O	N	F	L	R	U	H	D
E	D	I	E	L	S	N	I	A
N	T	A	R	A	U	C	D	M
U	T	R	I	F	O	N	S	I
E	B	O	I	L	I	N	G	A

Now **write the leftover letters,** in order from left to right, to find the meaning of "Wailuku."

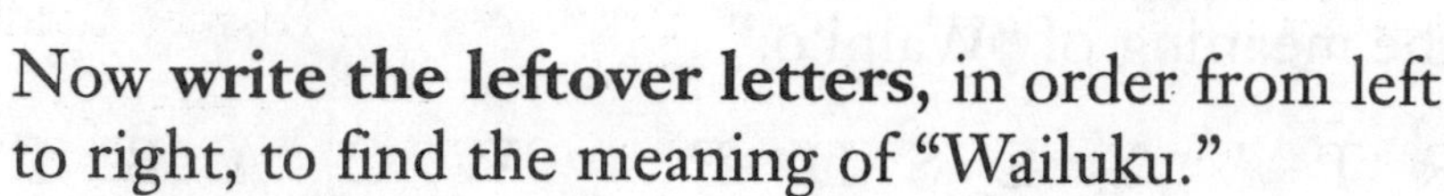

Waipi'o Valley

Waipi'o Valley on the Hāmākua Coast is a beautiful, deep valley with waterfalls and streams. Thousands of people once lived in this valley. A few families live here now and grow taro. Taro (called "*kalo*" in Hawaiian) is grown in soil that is flooded with water. Taro is important in the Hawaiian diet. It can be eaten in three ways: the root can be pounded into a paste called "poi," the young leaves can be cooked and eaten like spinach, and the root can also be cooked and eaten in chunks.

Find the following things hidden in the taro patch: bird, spider, fish, butterfly, poi pounder, duck, turtle, the words "taro," "poi," and "Waipi'o."

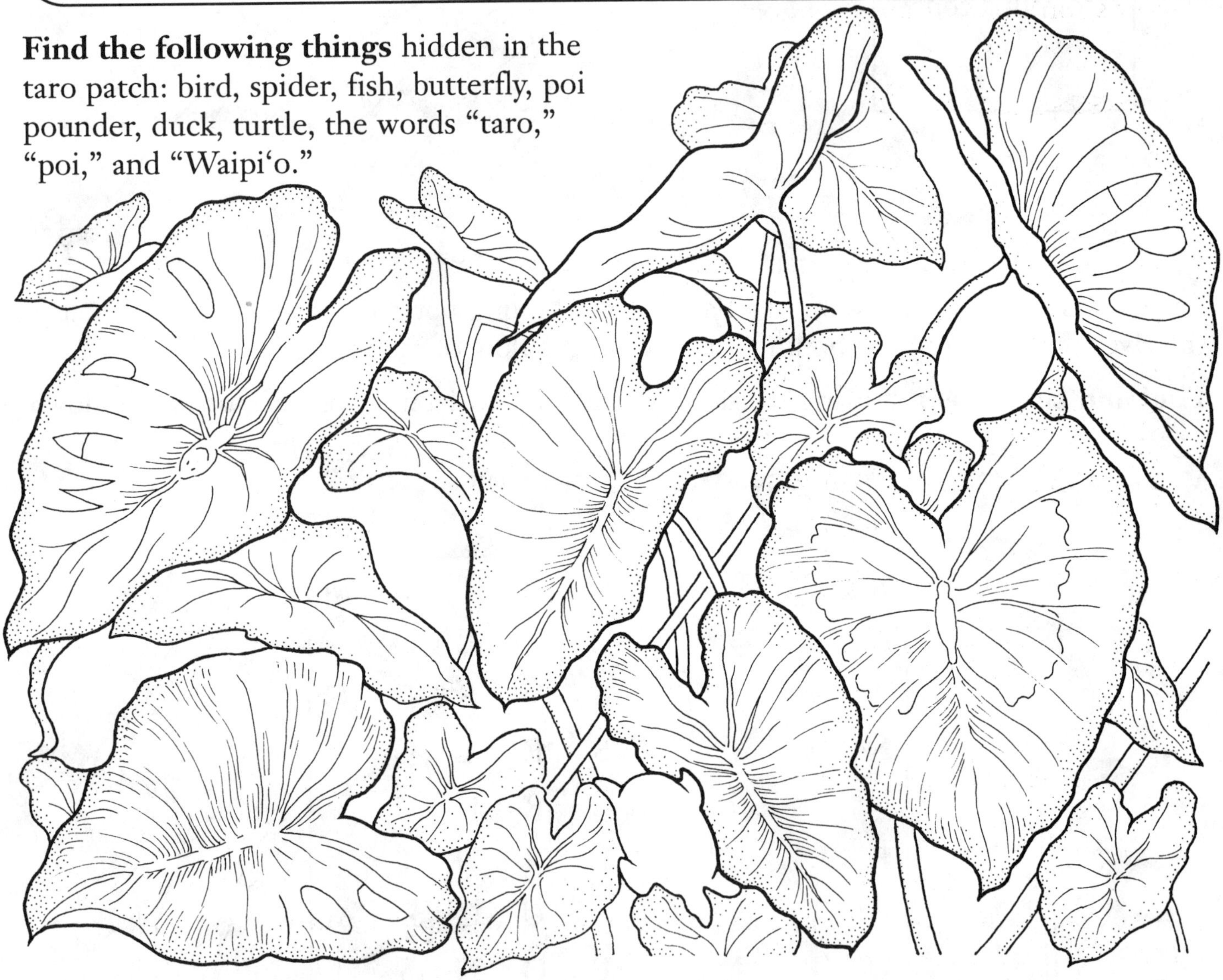

Mark out every other letter in the words below (follow the example). The remaining letters spell the meaning of "Waipi'o."

C X U P R T V Y E S D F   W O A B T U E C R

_ _ _ _ _ _ _   _ _ _ _ _

Waimea

The Waimea area of the Big Island has rolling green hills and open grassland. It is cowboy country. Kamehameha I received gifts of cows in 1793, and horses in 1828, and placed a *kapu* on hurting or killing them. When the herds grew so large that they became a danger to crops and people, the king hired Mexican and South American cowboys to teach Hawaiians how to manage the cattle. He also hired John Parker, who started the Parker Ranch, now one of the largest in the United States. The post office in Waimea town is called Kamuela. It means "Samuel" and may have been named for Samuel Parker (John Parker's son), or Samuel Spencer, a postmaster.

Circle the pictures that show things you would use as a cowboy or would need on a ranch.

| 1 = A |
| 2 = D |
| 3 = E |
| 4 = I |
| 5 = L |
| 6 = N |
| 7 = O |
| 8 = P |
| 9 = R |
| 10 = T |
| 11 = W |

Use this code to find the Hawaiian word for "cowboy." The word was actually Hawaiian for "Spanish" (referring to the Mexican and South American cowboys) but came to be commonly used for any cowboys.

___ ___ ___ ___ ___ ___ ___
 8 1 6 4 7 5 7

Now **use the same code** to learn what "Waimea" means. It was given this name because the streams were this color.

___ ___ ___   ___ ___ ___ ___ ___
 9 3 2   11 1 10 3 9

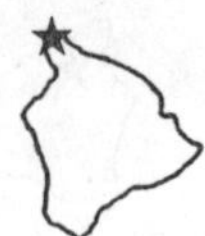

Kohala

King Kamehameha I was born in Kohala on the Big Island. He was the first Hawaiian ruler to conquer all the islands and became known as Kamehameha the Great. A statue of the king was made in Italy in 1880, but was lost in a shipwreck on the way to Honolulu. Another was made and now stands on King Street in Honolulu. Later, the original was found on the ocean floor and it stands at Kapa'au in North Kohala, the king's birthplace.

In the puzzle below, find the "path" of letters that correctly spell "King Kamehameha the Great."

K K K
I I I I
N N N N
G G G
K K K K K
A A A A A
M M M M M
E E E E E
H H H H A
M A A A H
E M M M A
H E E E E
A H M H M
H A E H E
A T T A H
G H H A A
R E E G H
E G G A E
A R A E T
T E A A T
A E
T

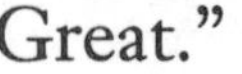

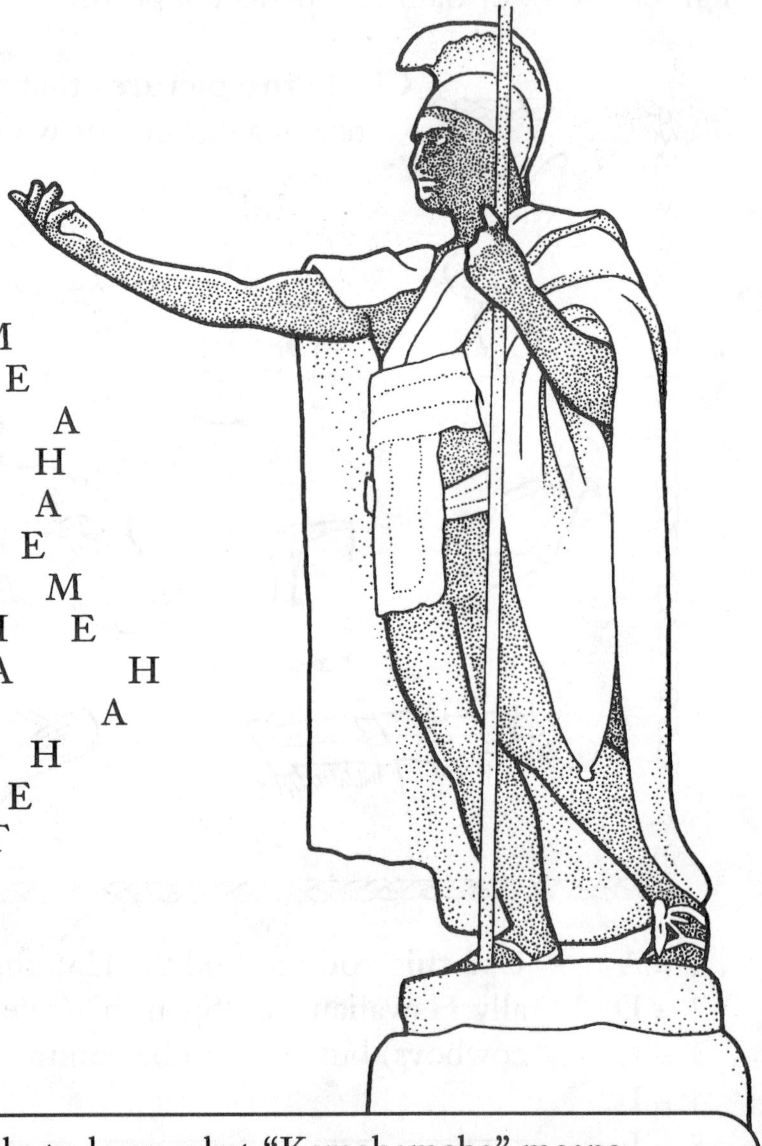

Use the code below to fill in the blanks to learn what "Kamehameha" means:

Y	N	T	E	L	H	O
1	2	3	4	5	6	7

___ ___ ___   ___ ___ ___ ___ ___ ___   ___ ___ ___
3 6 4   5 7 2 4 5 1   7 2 4

Kona

Every fall, humpback whales migrate to Hawai'i from Alaska to spend the winter months in warmer waters. The Kona Coast is one of their favorite places. A humpback whale can weigh as much as 100,000 pounds (50 tons) and can be up to 60 feet long.

Count by 2's to find out how many tons a humpback can weigh. The correct numbers may be vertical, horizontal, or diagonal.

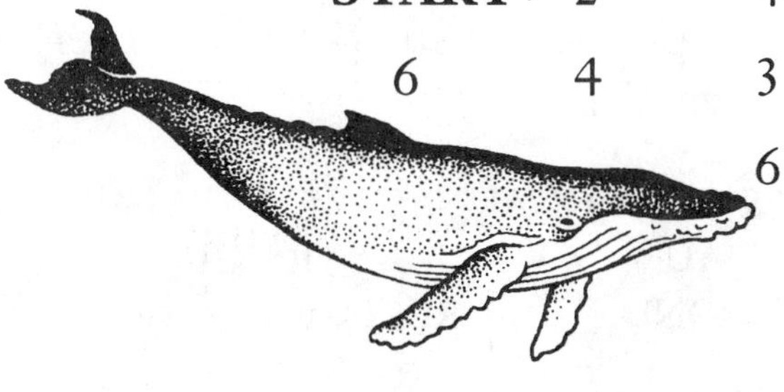

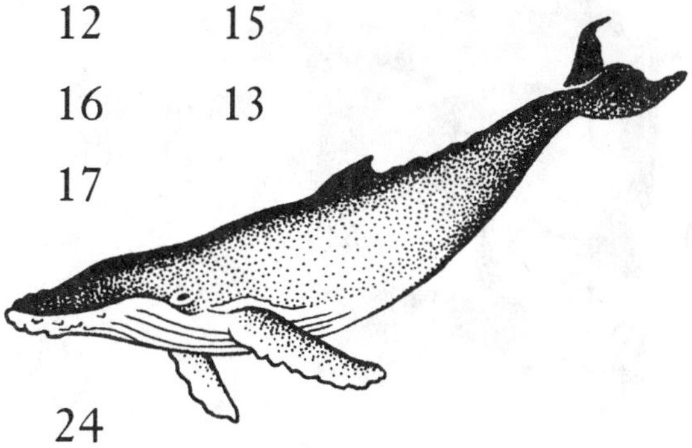

			4	3			
		START ▶ 2	4	5	10		
	6	4	3	7	8	9	
			6	8	10	12	15
				10	11	16	13
				12	14	17	
21	18	16	14	13	19		
17	19	18	18	21	22		
	23	20	22	20	19	24	
	24	25	20	23	26	28	30
			33	32	30	33	
			34	36	35	32	
				37	38	40	41
				40	44	42	44
				46	46	48	50

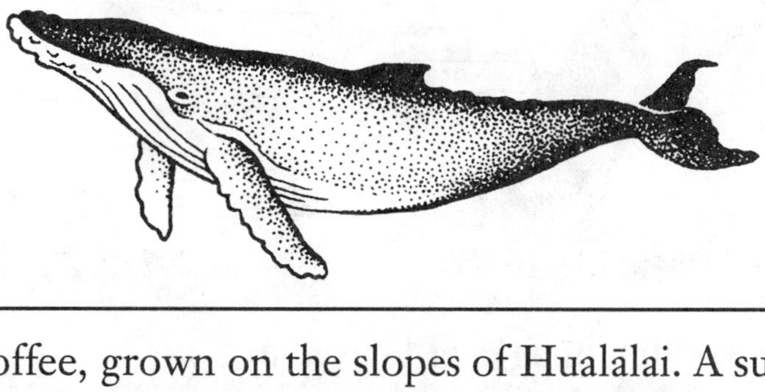

Kona is also known for its coffee, grown on the slopes of Hualālai. A summer home for royalty, Hulihe'e Palace, is in Kailua-Kona, where King Kamehameha I died in 1819, at Ahu'ena Heiau (temple).

Place of Refuge

Pu'uhonua-o-Hōnaunau ("place of refuge") is a national historical park. In old Hawai'i, many things were *kapu*, or against the law. If people who broke a *kapu* could get to a place of refuge before being caught, they would escape punishment or death.

At the refuge are palace grounds, a royal fish pond and canoe landing, a "great wall," which is 10 feet high, 17 feet wide, and more than 1000 feet long, and a *heiau* (temple), called Hale o Keawe.

Find the words listed below to reach the refuge and escape the king's warriors. The words in the puzzle are in the same order as listed. They are all horizontal or vertical.

1. HALE
2. KEAWE
3. CHIEFS
4. HONAUNAU
5. GREAT WALL
6. BONES
7. PUUHONUA
8. HEIAU
9. KAPU
10. KII
11. TEMPLE
12. IMAGES
13. FISH POND
14. REFUGE

```
                    H
              K E A W E
                P   L R
            C H I E F S
                O   S U B
              P N W A T R
        G R E A T W A L L   L
              V S U M R N
        W B O N E S
              N A C P S N
            P U U H O N U A
              T E K A R
              S R I C U
              W A B
        O K A P U
          I B N R T
          I M A G E S
          S T V M E B
        - F I S H P O N D
          G R E L V
        R E F U G E
```

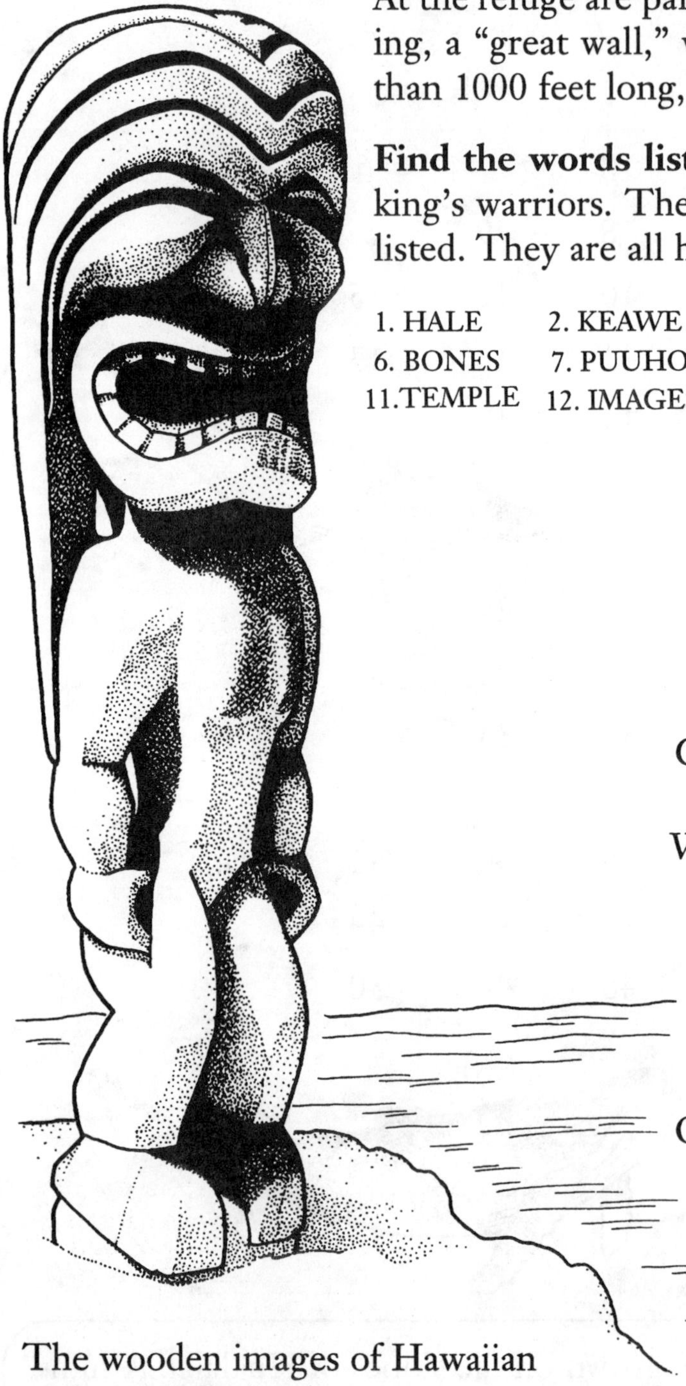

The wooden images of Hawaiian gods are called *ki'i*.

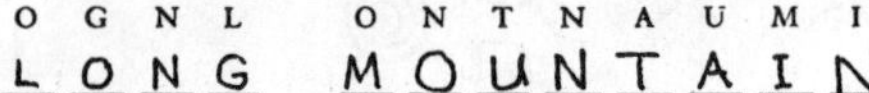

LONG MOUNTAIN

Kilauea is the Big Island's youngest volcano. **Follow the lines below to find out what "Kilauea" means.**

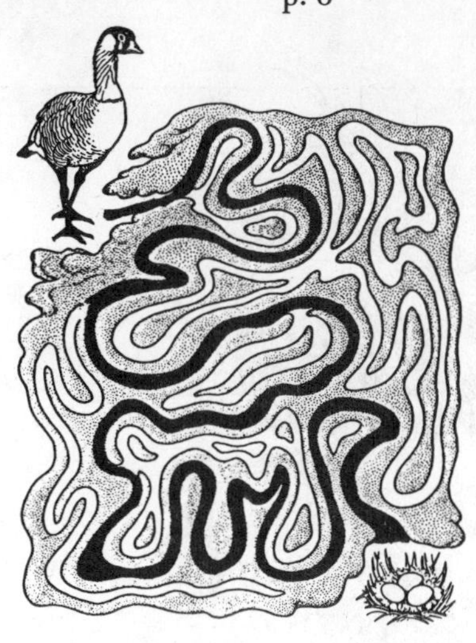

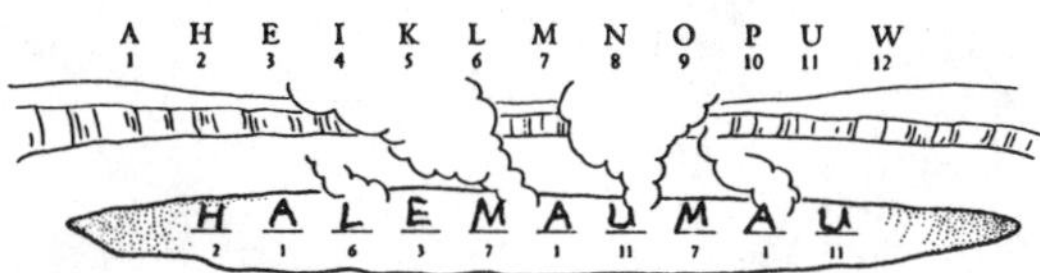

Now match the numbers and letters again to learn what this name means in English.

The crater is also known as the home of Pele, the Hawaiian goddess of fire.

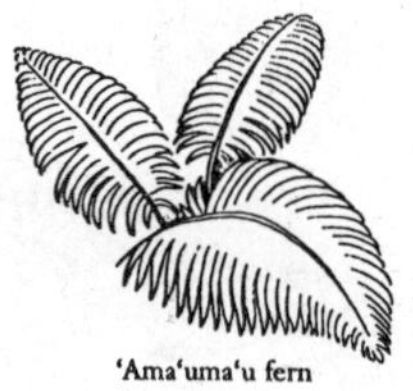
'Ama'uma'u fern

The *lehua* blossom is the flower of the native *'ōhi'a* tree. Legends say that if you pick a blossom going up the volcano, it will rain. Even if you're going downhill, don't pick the flowers. They provide food for native forest birds.

The pretty little bamboo orchid is not native to Hawai'i. It grows near the sulphur banks and steaming bluffs. The flower is purple, lavender, and white.

Mountain *naupaka* is a "half" flower with only five petals. It is usually white. The little fruits it forms are a very dark purple. There is also a *naupaka* at sea level. A legend says that two sweethearts were separated and one became the half flower at the ocean and the other in the mountains.

'Ōhelo berries grow on a low bush. The red berries are a favorite food of *nēnē*.

Three kinds of ginger plants grow in the volcanoes area: white, yellow and kāhili (also yellow). They are very pretty and have a wonderful scent. However, they multiply rapidly and are choking out the native forest plants.

lehua bamboo orchid mountain naupaka 'ōhelo berries ginger

f i n	This is found on a fish.
f i t s	The right size (The shoe f_ _ _.)
f o o t	You walk on these (singular).
n o t	I will __ __ __ step on the footprints.
p i t	Hole in the ground
p o t	A big pan
p r i n t	To write or stamp
p r o o f	Evidence of truth or fact
r i p	To tear apart
r o o f	Top of a house
r o o t	Part of a plant that is underground
r o t	To decay or spoil
s o f t	Not hard or rough (A pillow is s _ _ _.)
s o n	A boy is this to his father.
s t o o p	To bend over
s t o p	To quit or halt
t i p	Pointed end or to turn something over
t o n	2000 pounds
t o o t	Noise from a horn or train
t o p	Highest part of something
t r i p	A journey or to stumble
t r o o p	A group of Scouts or soldiers
t r o t	Movement of a horse

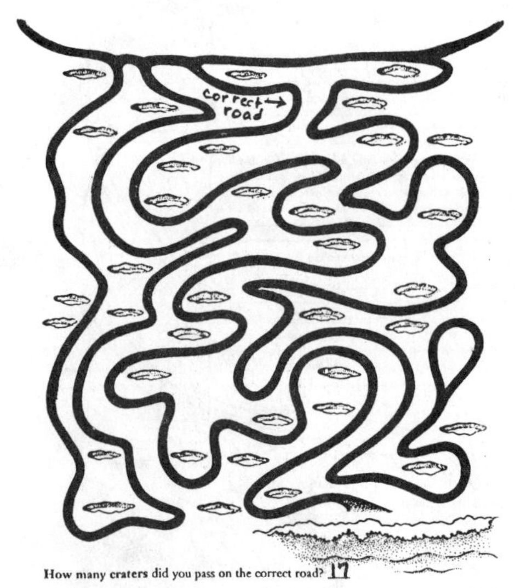

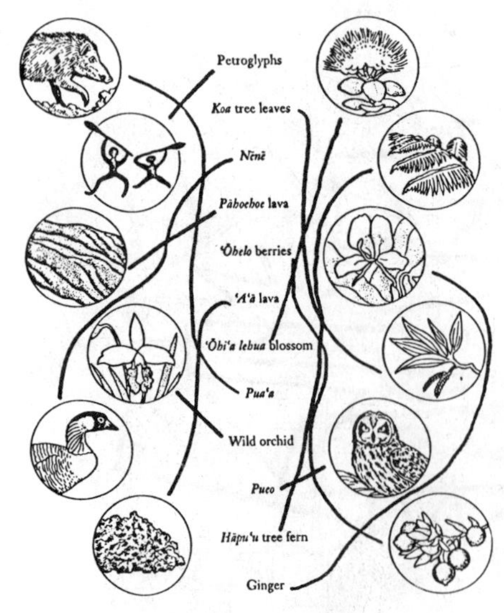

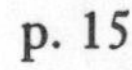

p. 15

p. 18

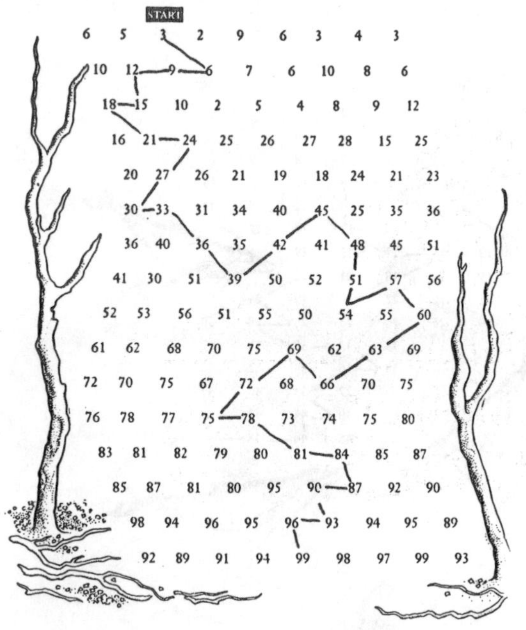

p. 19

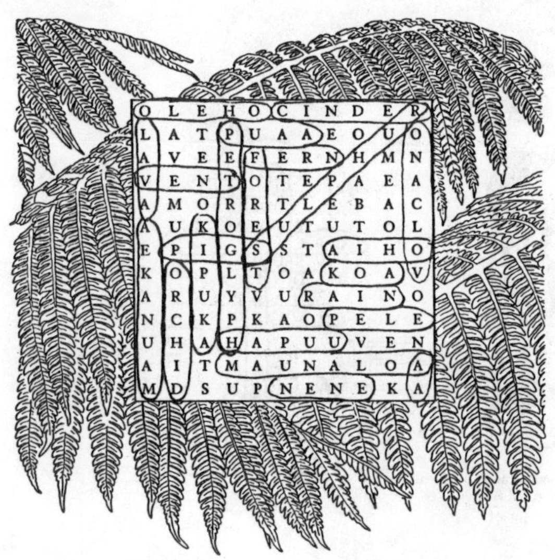

p. 20

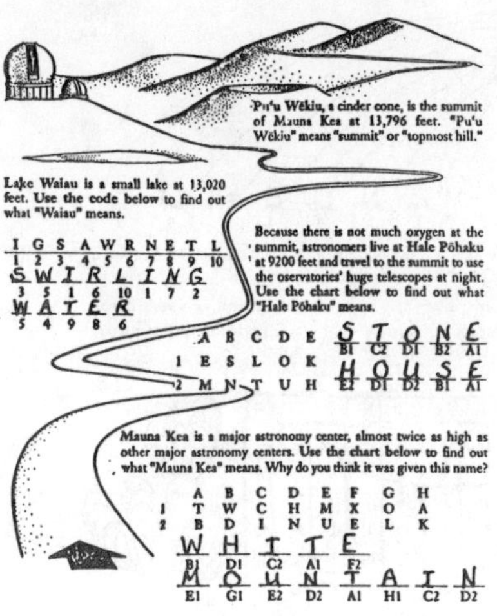

p. 21

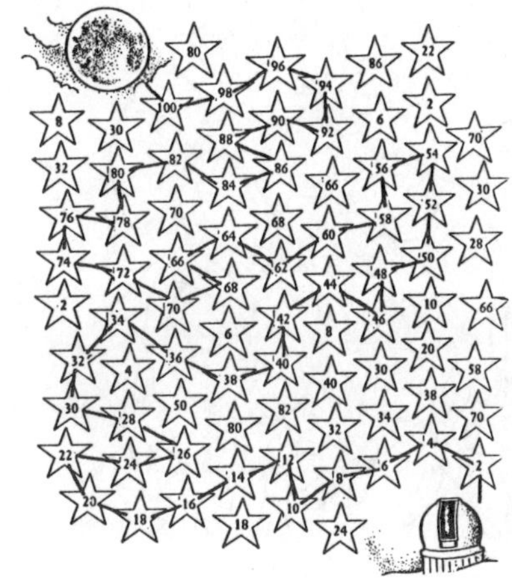

p. 22

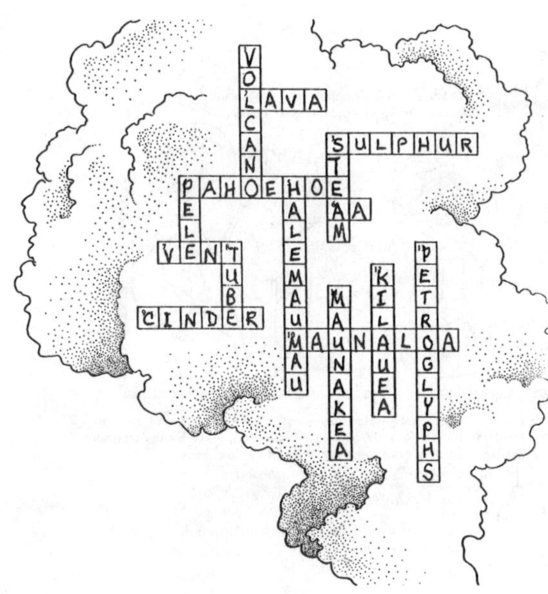

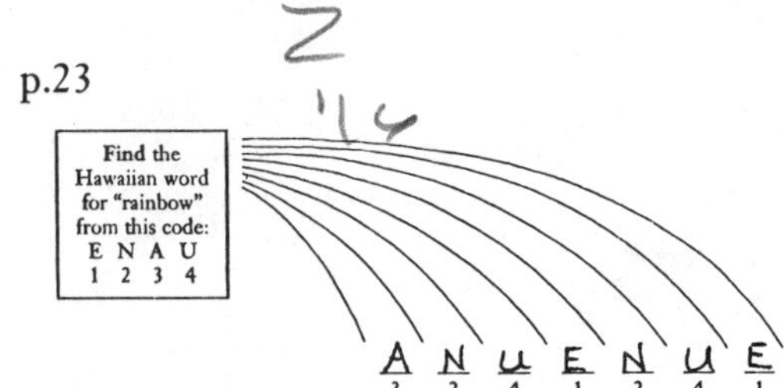

Farther up the river past Rainbow Falls are the boiling pots. They are a series of holes in the river that bubble like "boiling pots" when the flow of water is heavy.

Find and circle the following words. They may be horizontal, vertical, or upside down.

| POTS | BOILING | FALLS | RIVER | ORCHIDS | ANTHURIUM |
| MACADAMIA | RAINBOW | NUTS | ANUENUE | HILO | |

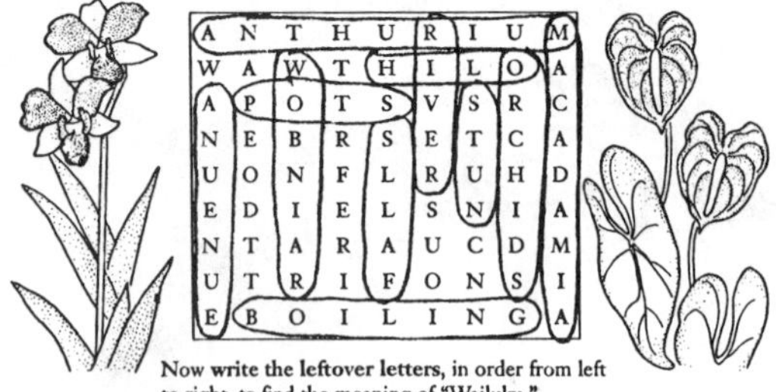

Now write the leftover letters, in order from left to right, to find the meaning of "Wailuku."

WATER OF DESTRUCTION

Find the following things hidden in the taro patch: bird, spider, fish, butterfly, poi pounder, duck, turtle, the words "taro," "poi," and "Waipi'o."

Mark out every other letter in the words below (follow the example). The remaining letters spell the meaning of "Waipi'o."

C X U P R T V Y E S D F   W O A B T U E C R
CURVED   WATER

Circle the pictures that show things you would use as a cowboy or would need on a ranch.

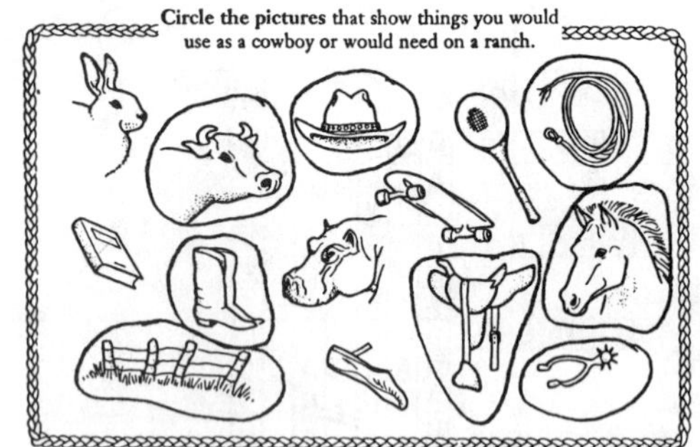

1 = A
2 = D
3 = E
4 = I
5 = L
6 = N
7 = O
8 = P
9 = R
10 = T
11 = W

Use this code to find the Hawaiian word for "cowboy." The word was actually Hawaiian for "Spanish" (referring to the Mexican and South American cowboys) but came to be commonly used for any cowboys.

PANIOLO
8 1 6 4 7 5 7

Now use **the same code** to learn what "Waimea" means. It was given this name because the streams were this color.

RED WATER
9 3 2   11 1 10 3 9

Use the code below to fill in the blanks to learn what "Kamehameha" means:

Y N T E L H O
1 2 3 4 5 6 7

THE LONELY ONE
3 6 4   5 7 2 4 5 1   7 2 4

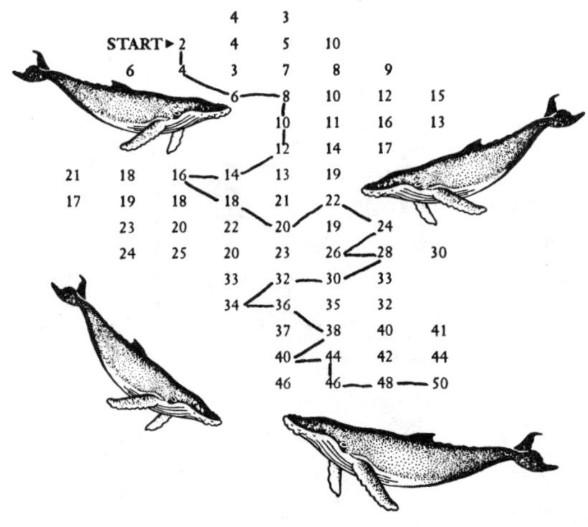

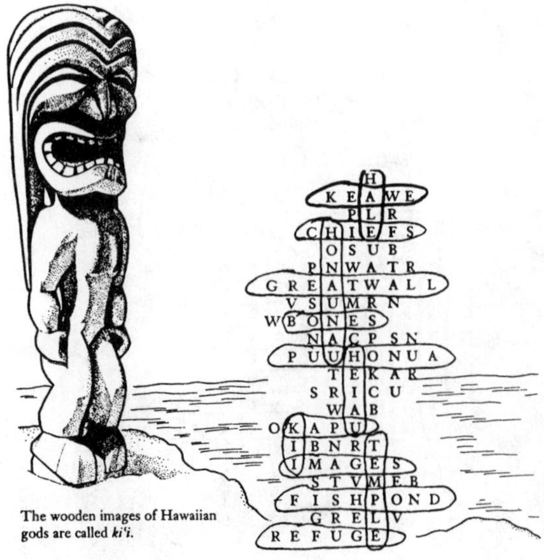

The wooden images of Hawaiian gods are called ki'i.